The Super Duper Princess Heroes

How It All Started

by

Sanjay Nambiar

To Zaara, Riya, Miya, Uma, and awesome girls everywhere.

Special thanks to:
Priya Nambiar, Nilesh Kapse, Alyssa Williamson, Prateek Sethi, Shreya Gulati, Ravi Asnani, Venu Alagh, Jeannine Jacobi, Sean Ross, Heidi Ross, Christina Kim, and our parents & siblings.

Edited by Priya Nambiar.
Designed and Printed by 3-Keys Communications.

First Edition | 10 9 8 7 6 5 4 3 2 1
ISBN 978-0-9838243-9-8
Library of Congress Control Number 2013931015

Printed in China.

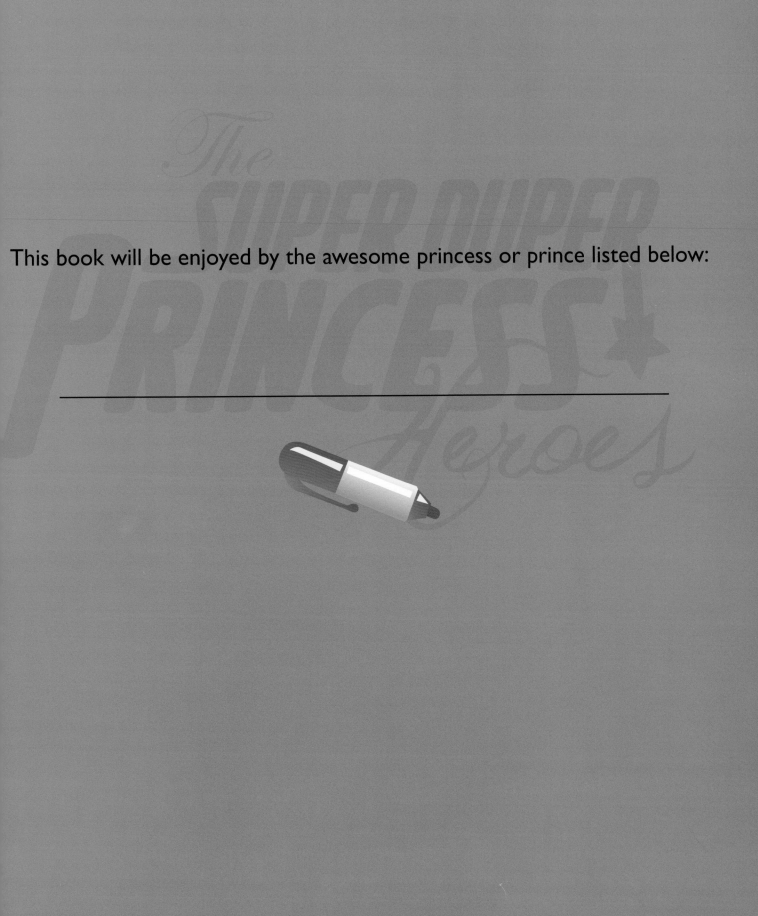

This book will be enjoyed by the awesome princess or prince listed below:

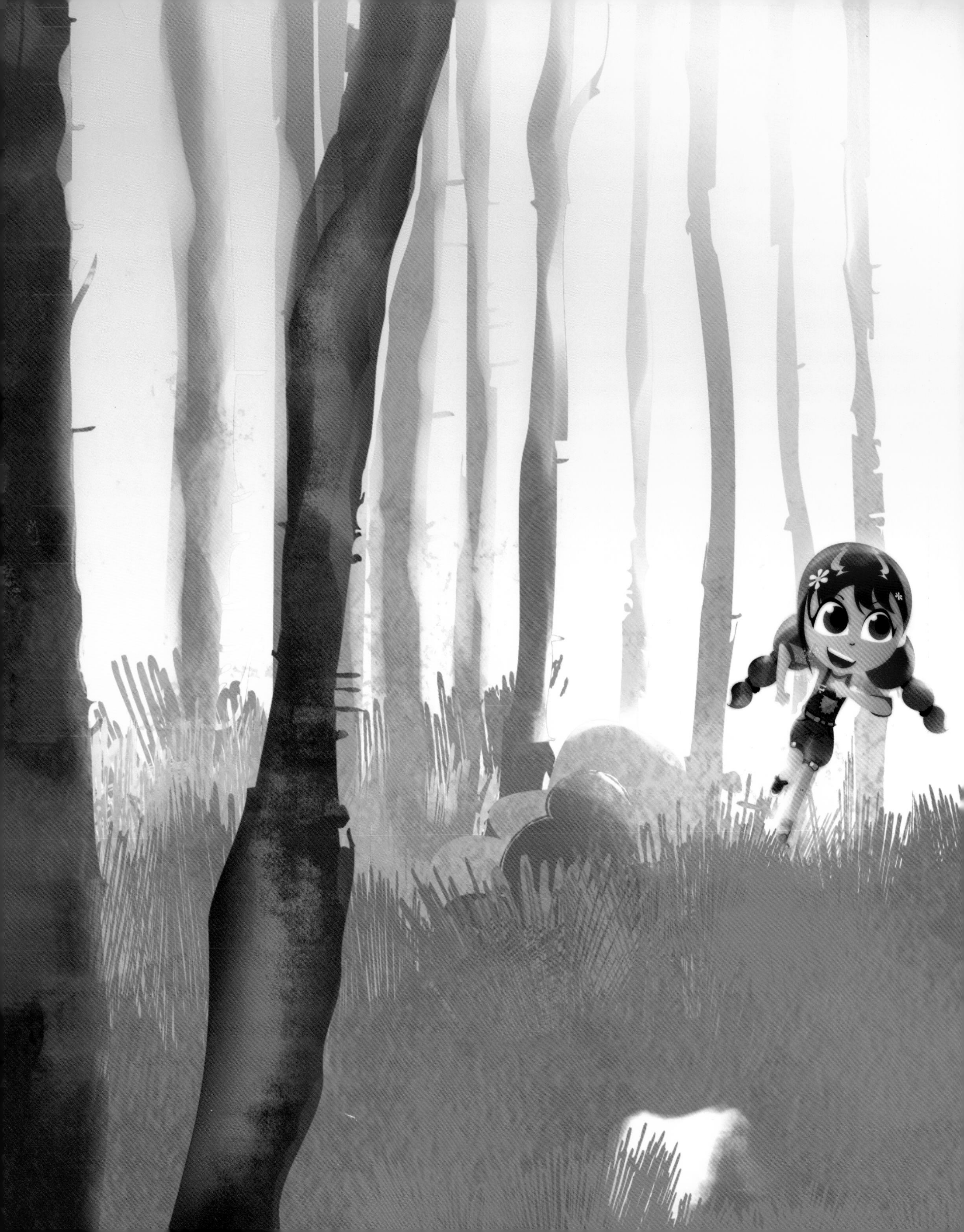

Not that long ago, in a magical place not far from where you are right now, three girls were playing in the woods.

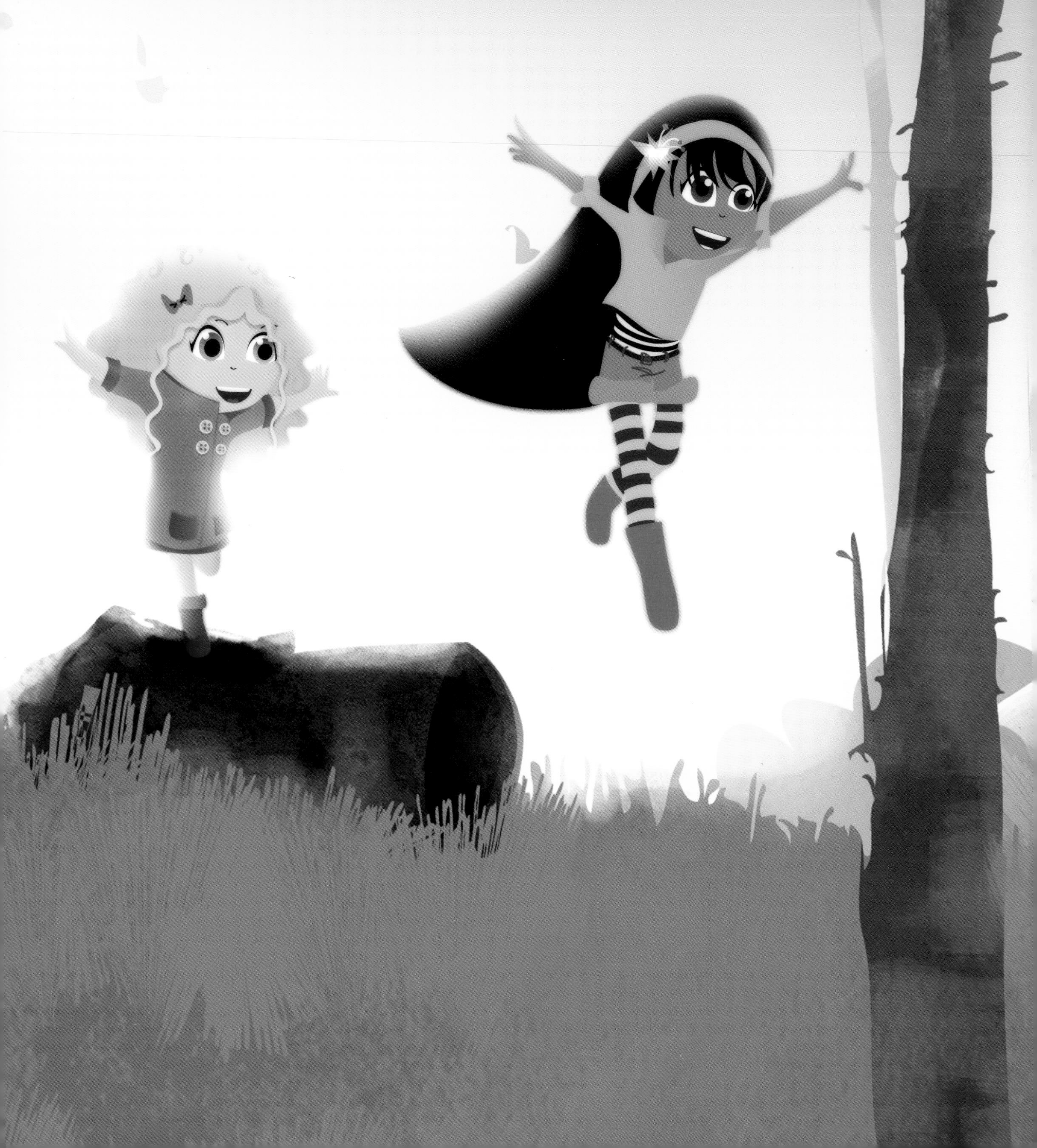

One of the girls, Oceana, found a strange, silver bag.

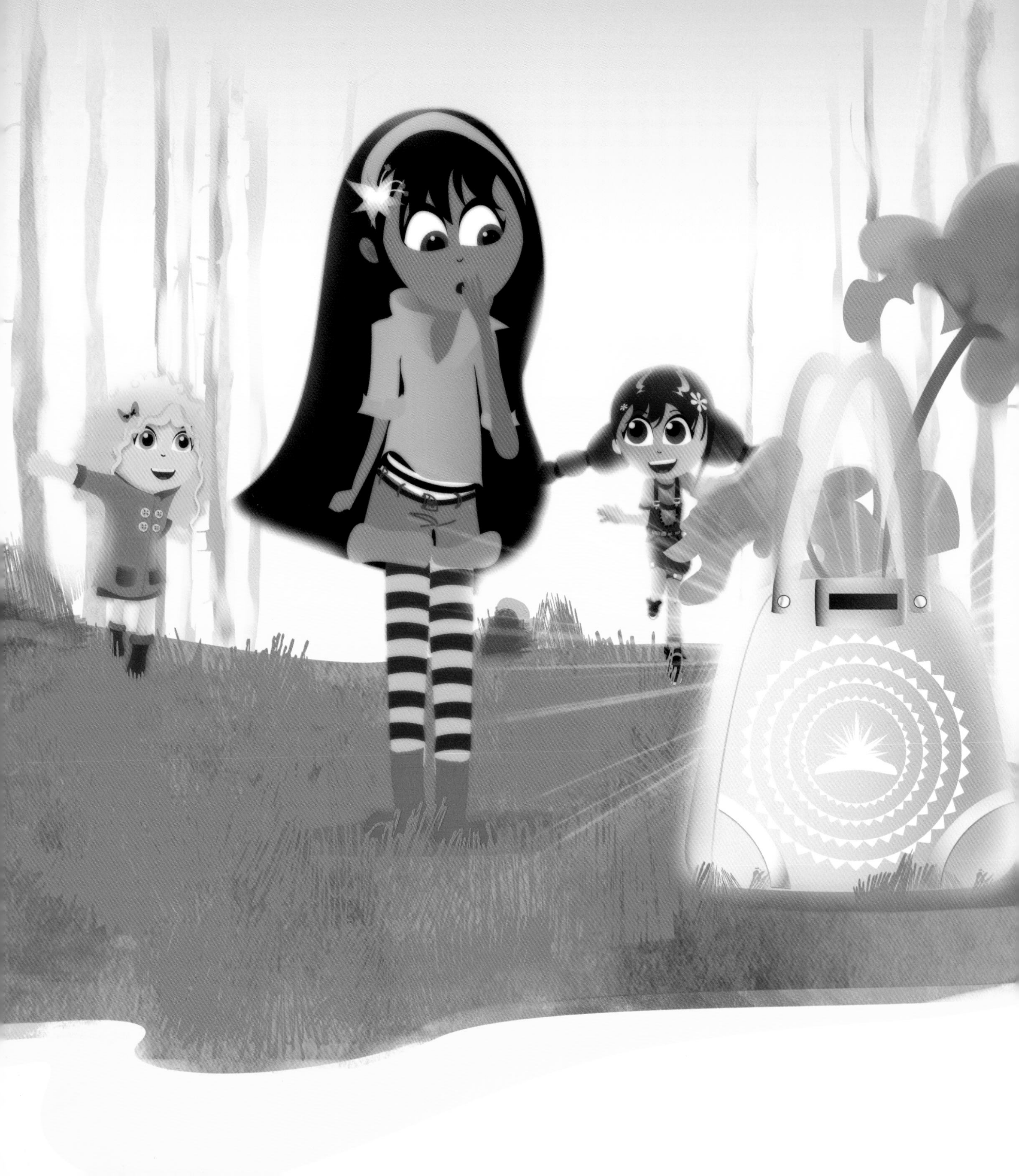

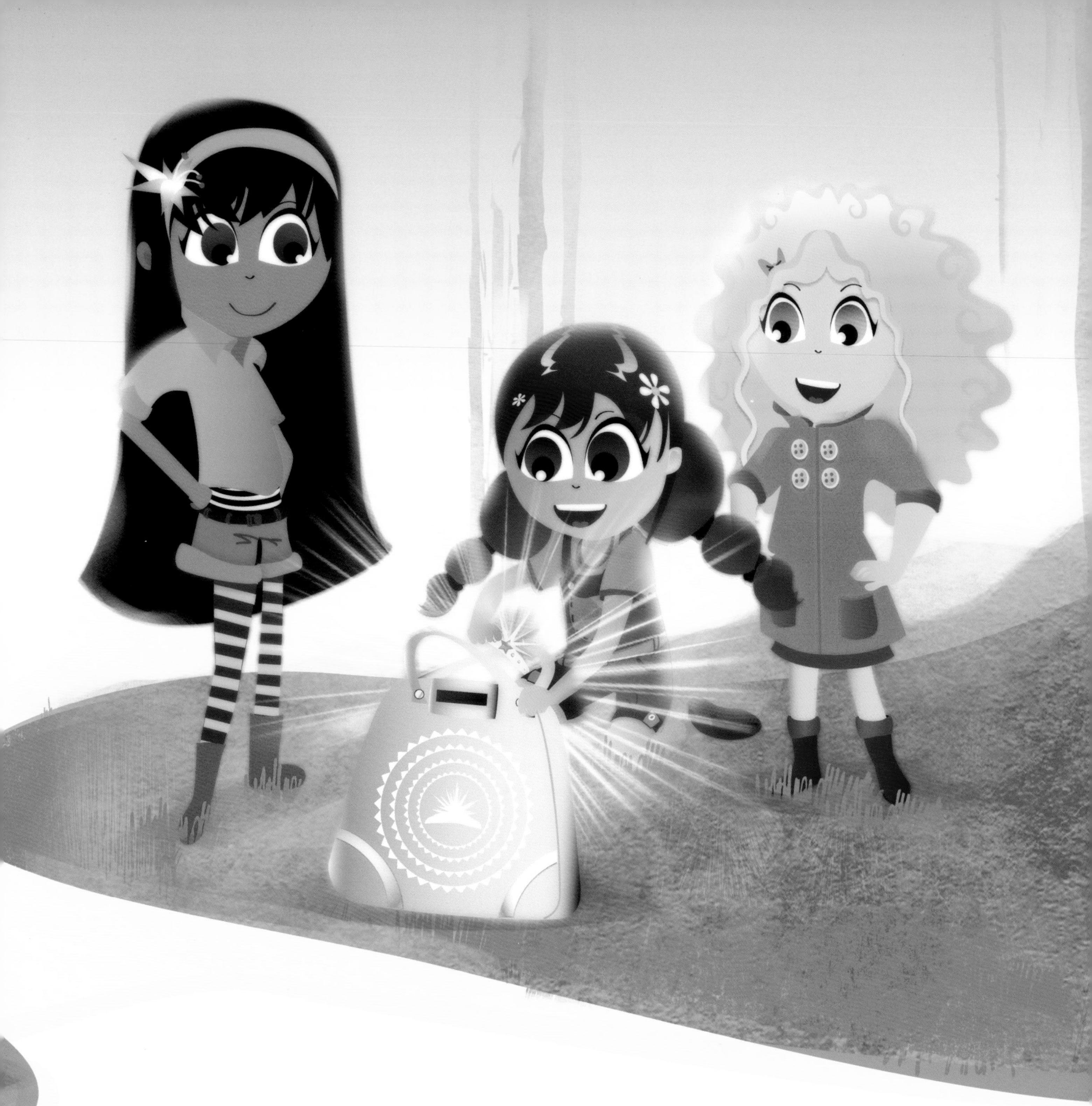

It seemed out of place, yet the girls were mysteriously drawn to it.

Sammie and Oceana watched as Kinney slowly looked inside, where she found . . .

. . . three glittering *tiaras*.
The girls put them on and a fabulous whirl of glitter and sparkles suddenly engulfed them!

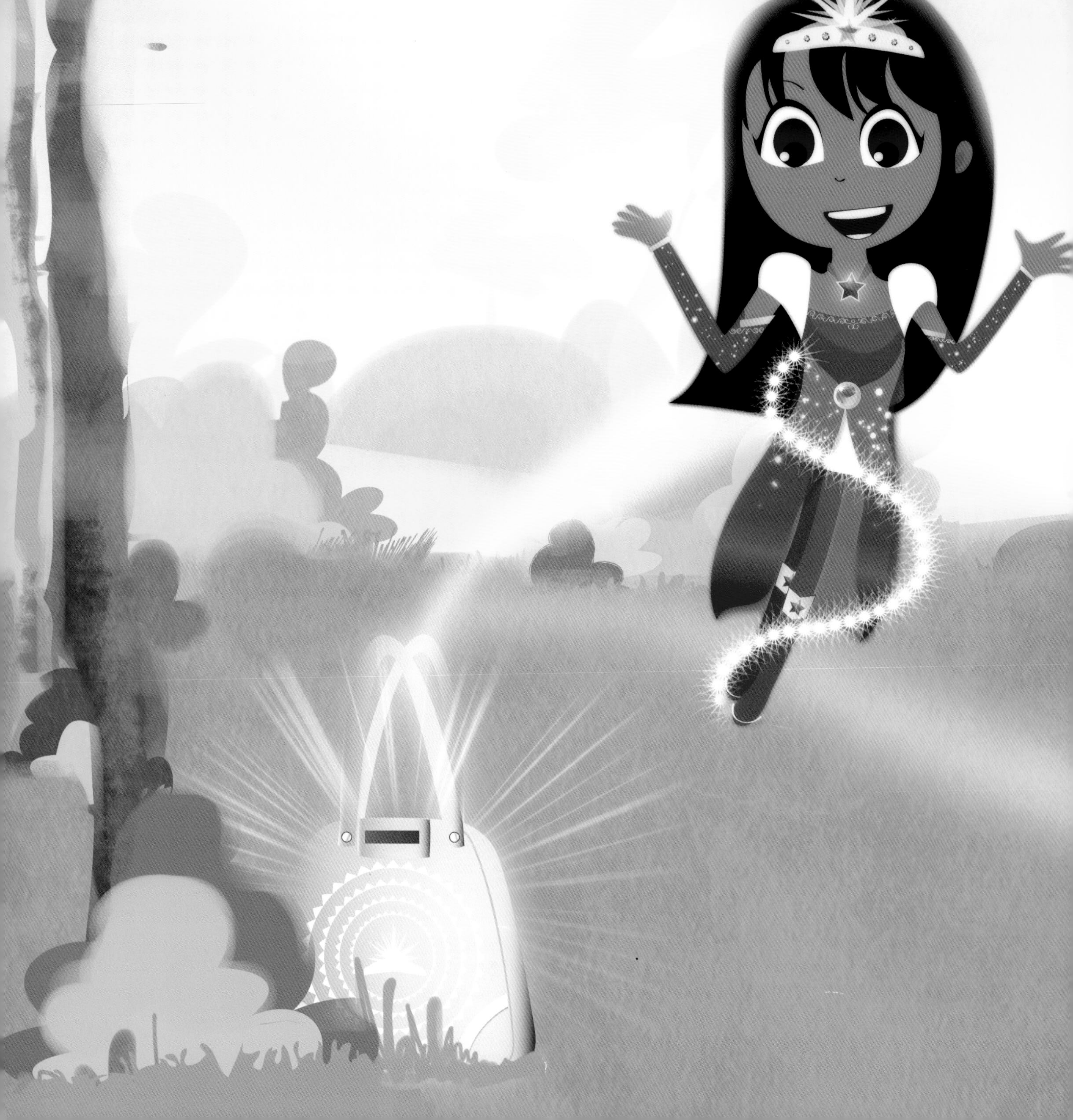

Their regular clothes turned into amazing gowns.
Lovely lavenders, gorgeous greens, terrific tangerines.
It was like a rainbow of awesomeness!

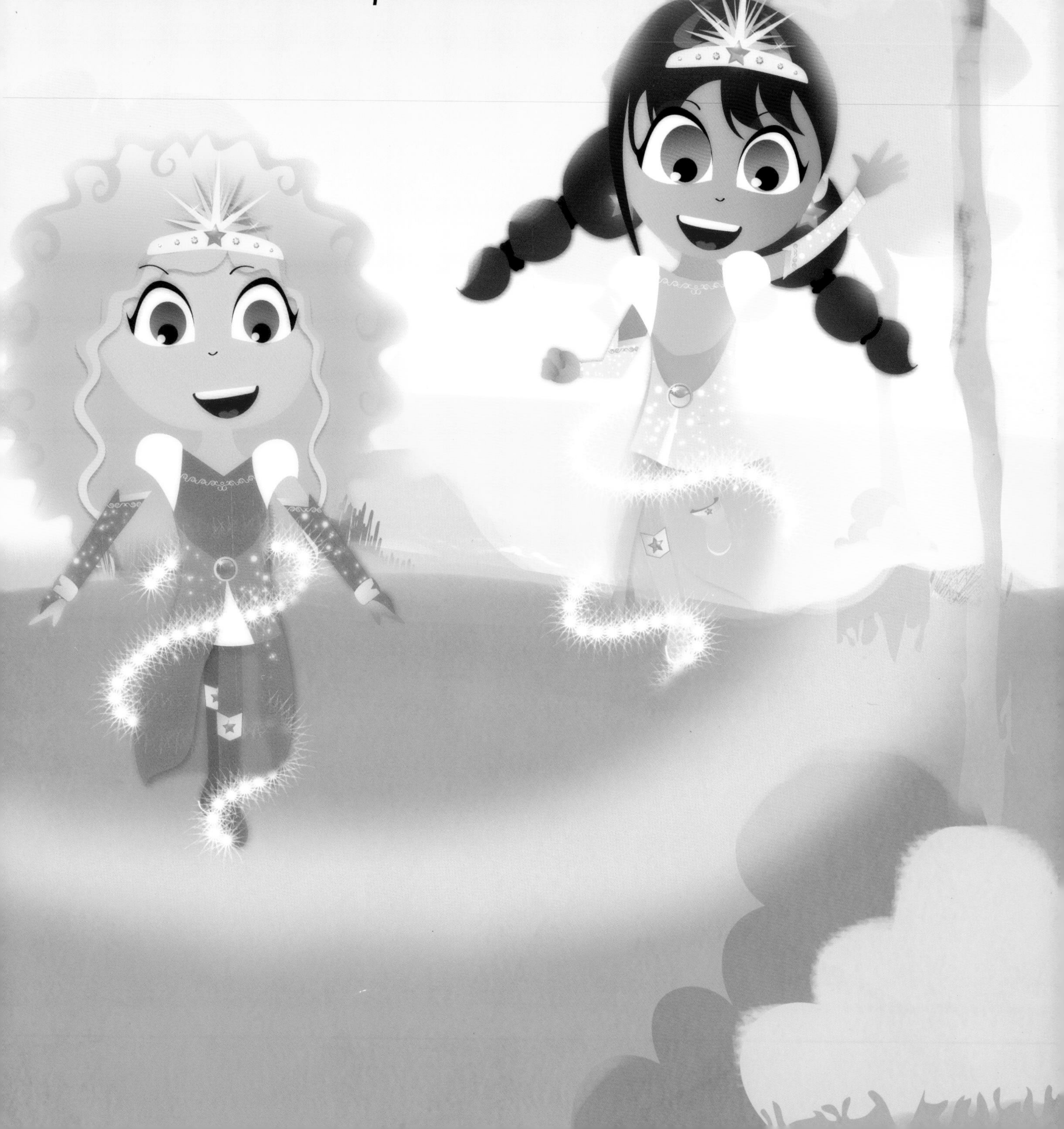

A cloud of smoke emerged from the bag.
A beautiful lady stepped forward.

She was the ***Fairy Teacher Mother Superstar Queen***.
Her name was Betty.

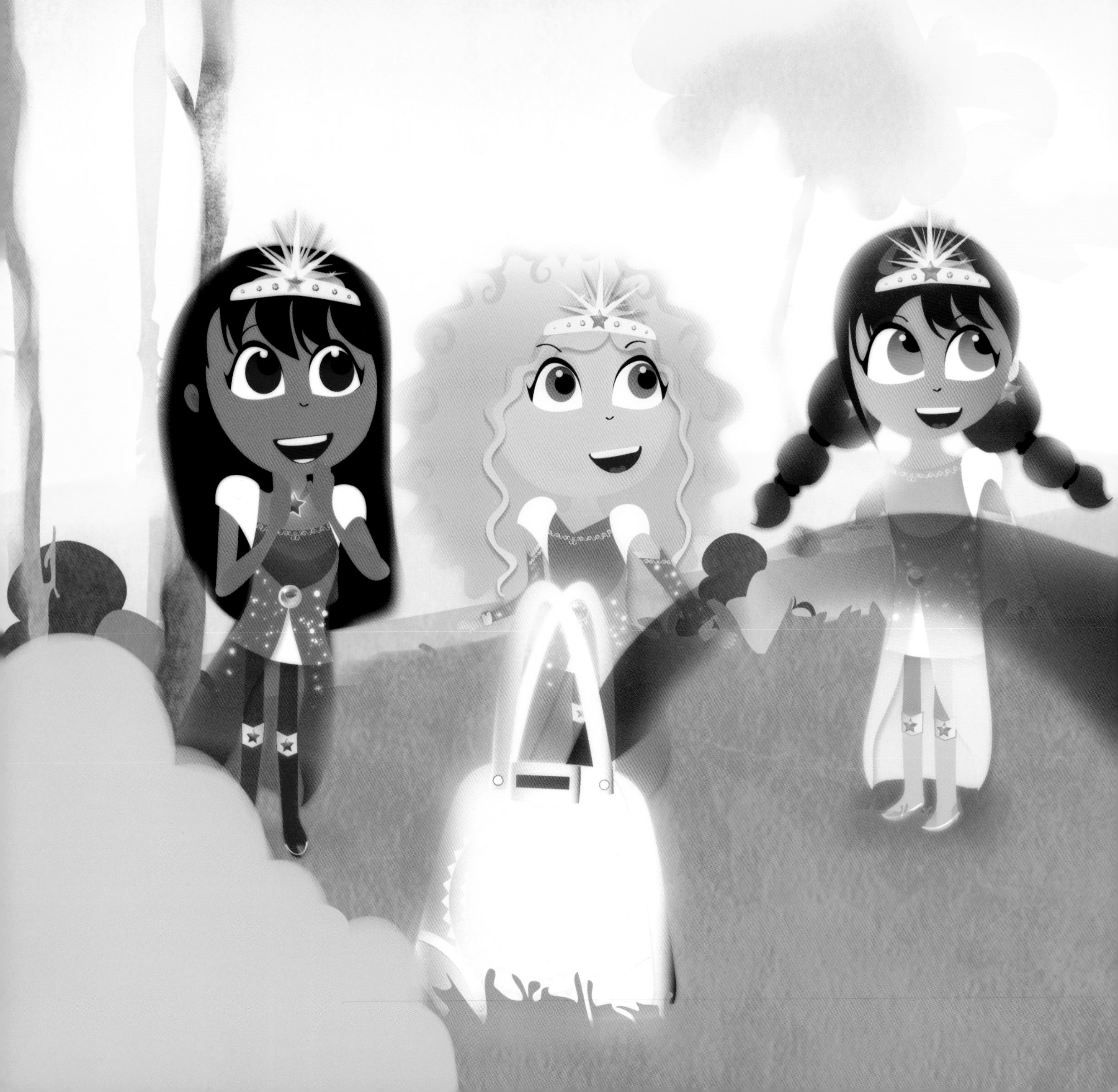

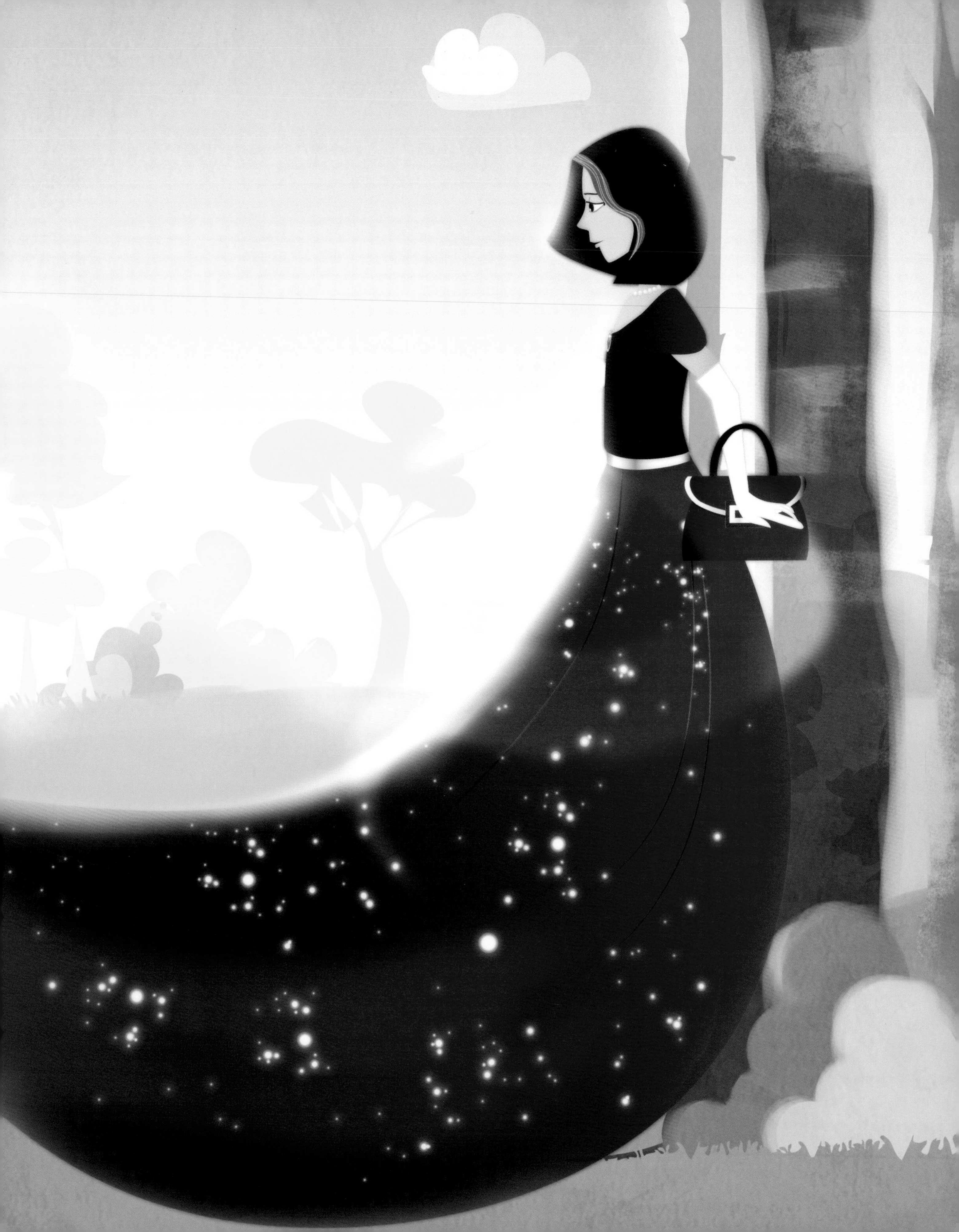

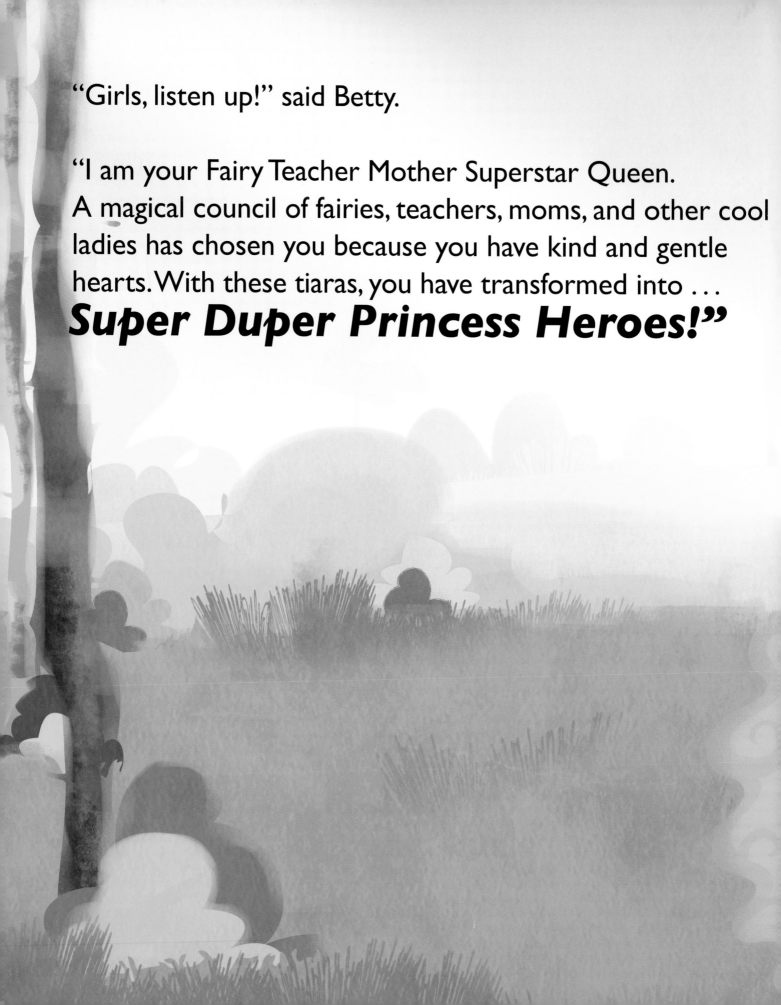

"Girls, listen up!" said Betty.

"I am your Fairy Teacher Mother Superstar Queen.
A magical council of fairies, teachers, moms, and other cool
ladies has chosen you because you have kind and gentle
hearts. With these tiaras, you have transformed into . . .
Super Duper Princess Heroes!"

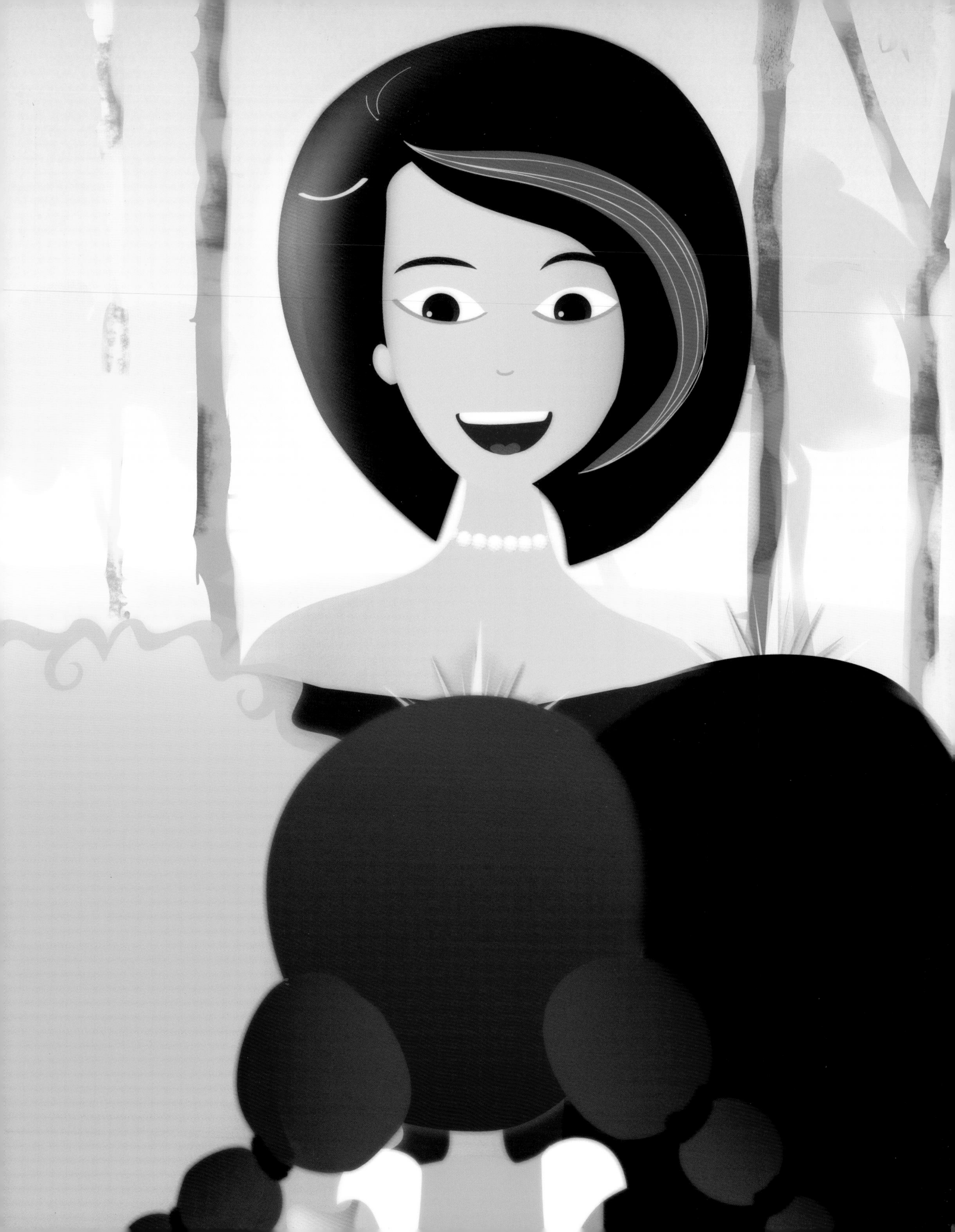

Kinney looked at Betty in surprise and awe.
"What in the world is a *Super Duper Princess Hero?*" she asked.

"Good question," replied Betty. "You now have super powers. Kinney, you have the power of speed. You can run like the wind, only faster and with better direction. Sammie, you have the power of strength. You can pick up giant boulders like they were tiny pebbles. Just look where you throw them—giant boulders can really hurt other people. Oceana, you have the power of flight. Soar as high as you want, but watch out for tall trees and pokey branches."

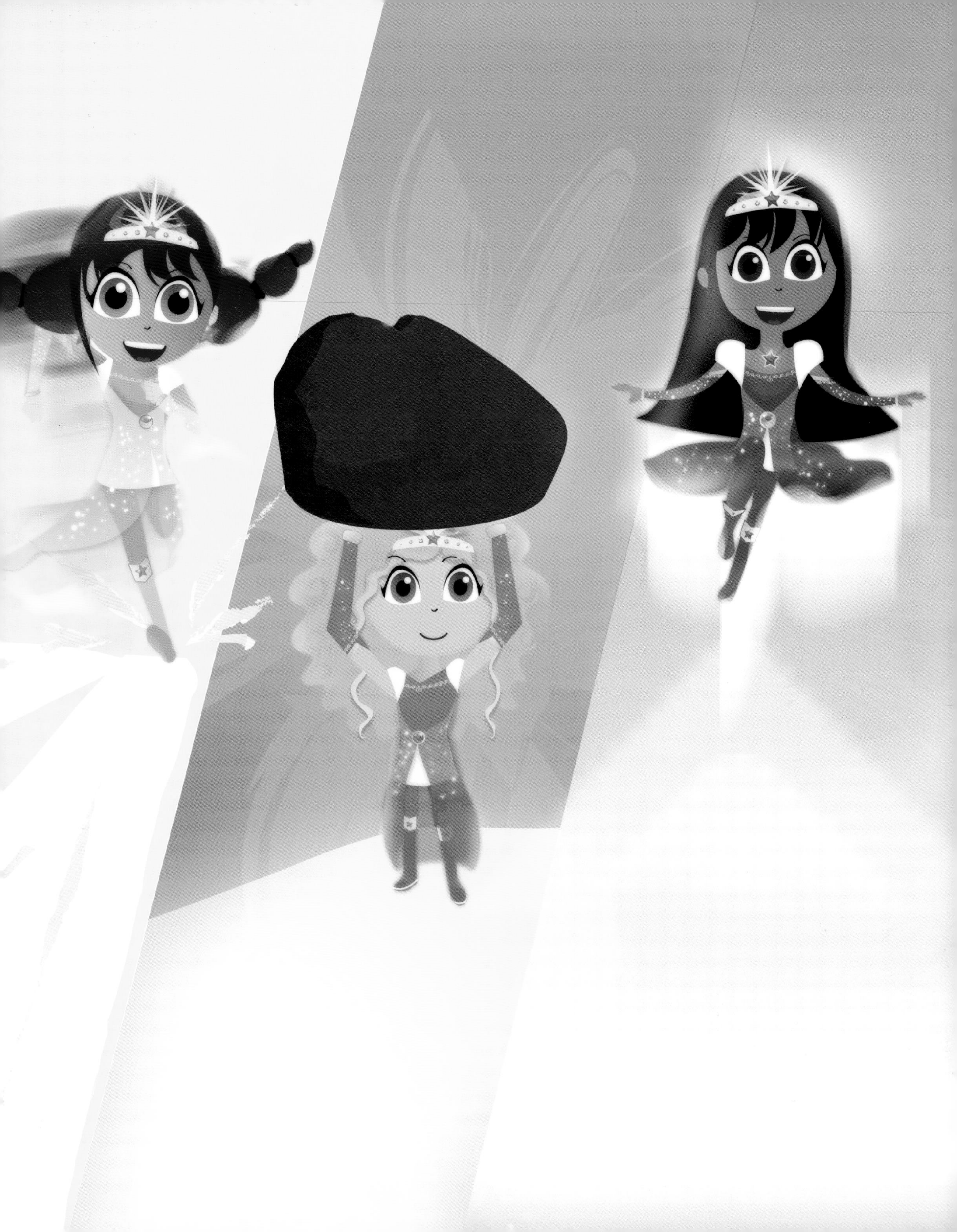

"You only have super powers when you wear the tiaras, which were designed especially for each of you. Once you take the tiaras off, no more super powers. Get it? Good.

But here's the most important part: the tiaras work only under three conditions.

1) You must be kind and use your powers to help others;
2) You must work together as a team whenever you can; and,
3) You must be humble and never arrogant about your powers.

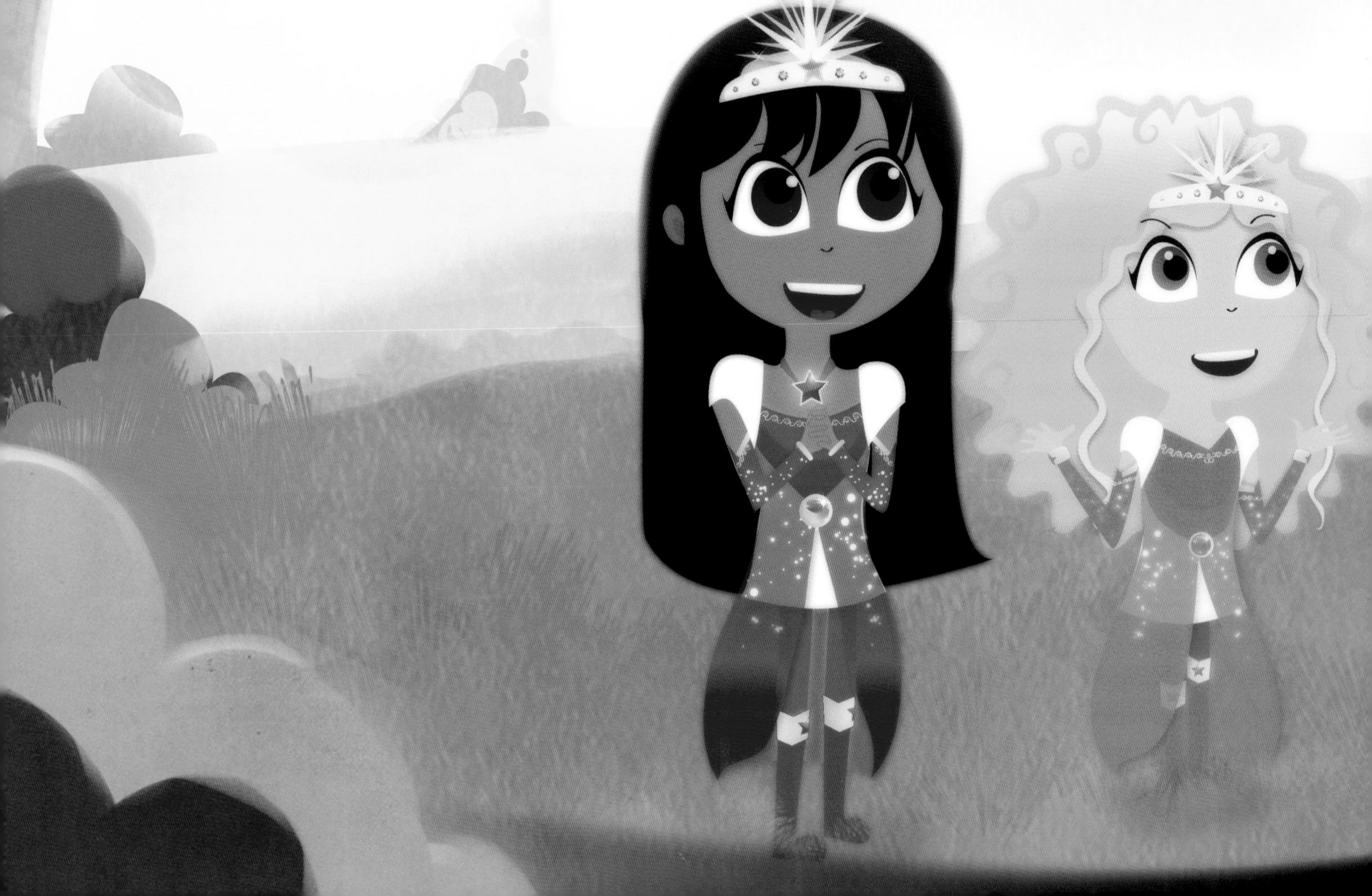

Good luck, my lovely princesses!"

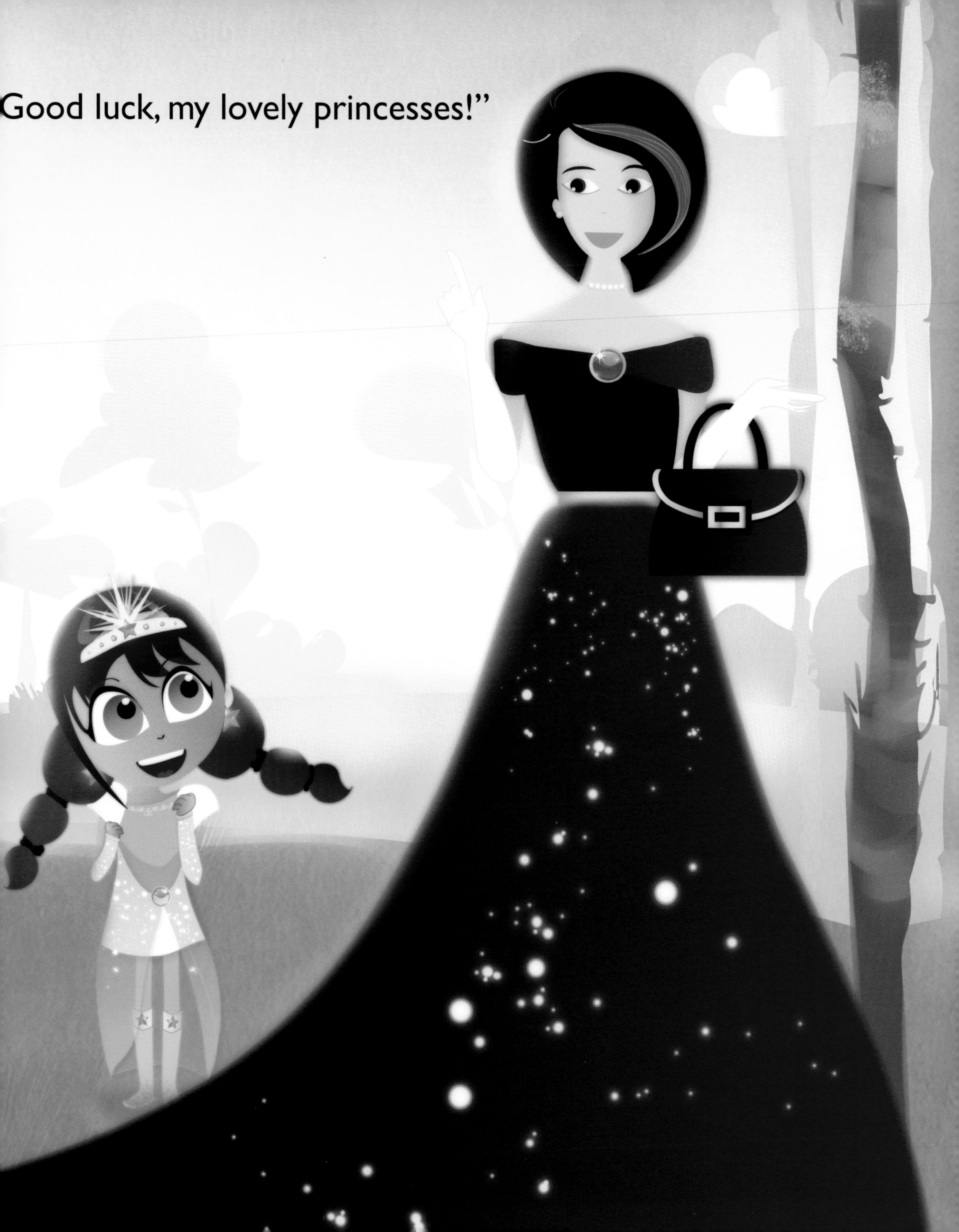

Betty vanished in a swirl of smoke, as did the strange, silver bag. Before the girls could look for her, however, they heard a loud scream.

"Oh no!" shouted Kinney.
"Sounds like someone's in trouble!"

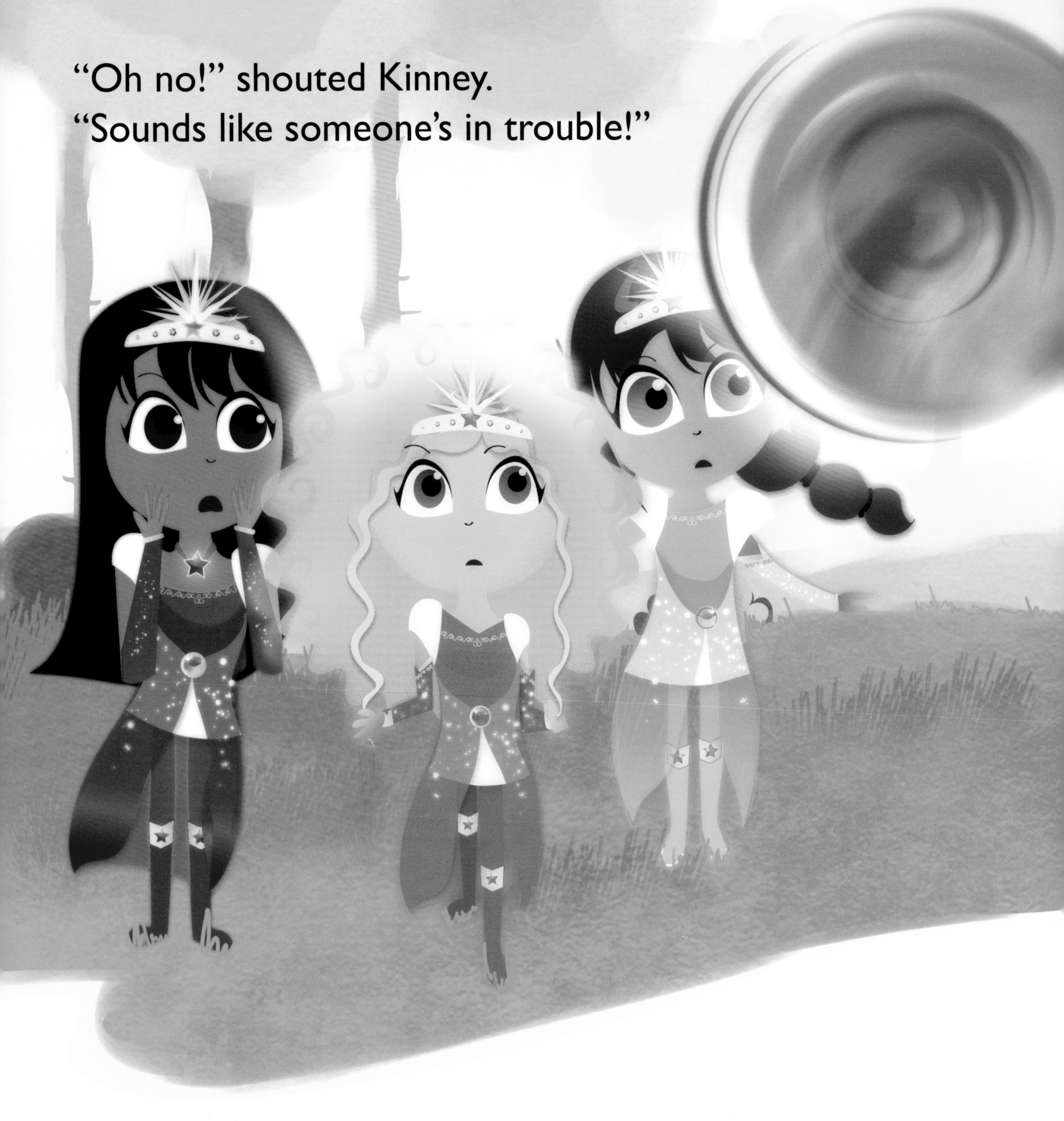

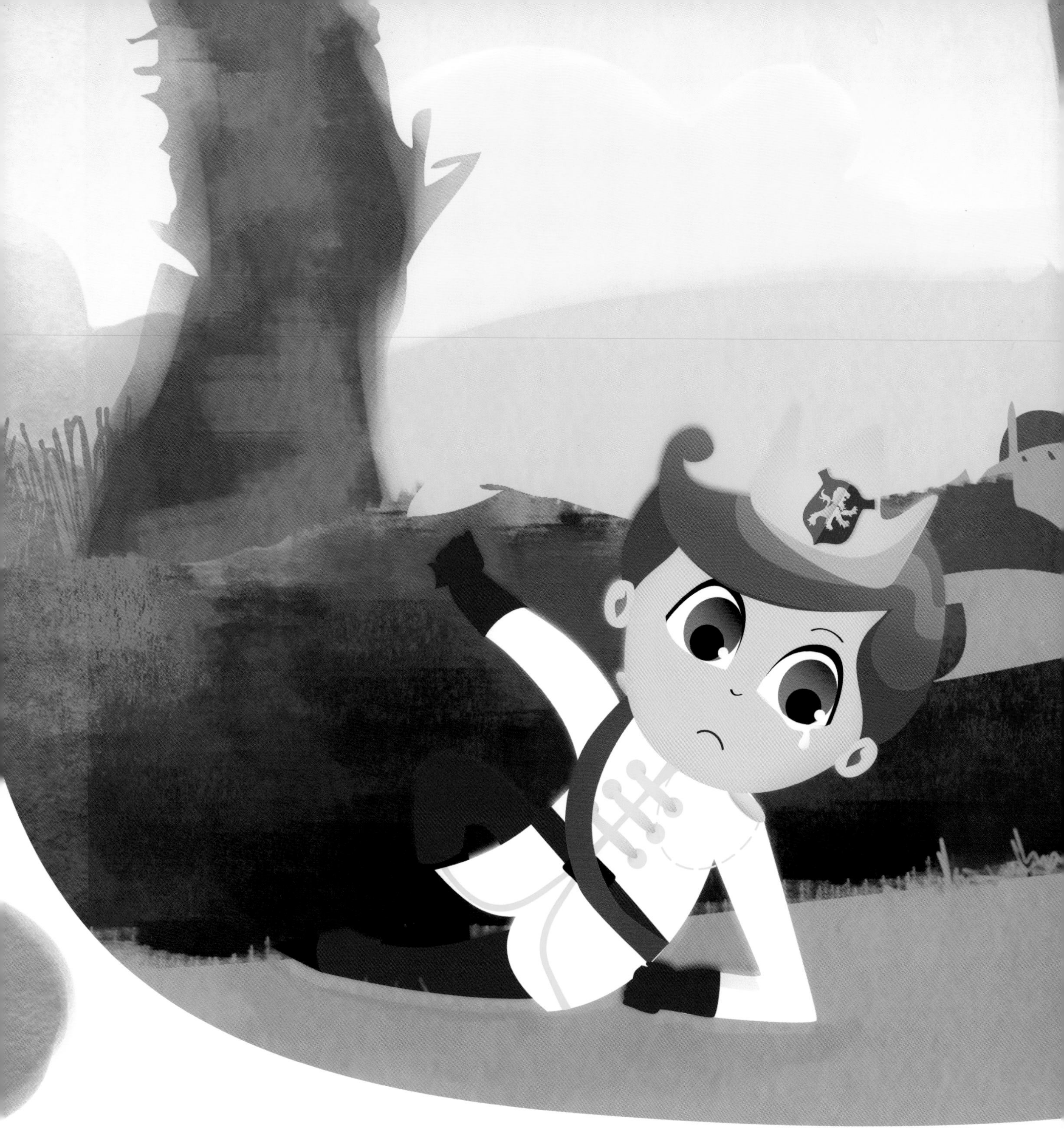

The girls ran toward the noise and found a boy next to a river. He was wearing a gold crown and a fancy suit with sashes—quite an unusual outfit for someone in the forest.

"Please help me!" said the boy.

"Wait a second," said Kinney. "I recognize you. You're Prince Felipe from the neighboring kingdom!"

"My leg really hurts and I can't move this tree. I need to go home and it's getting dark," said Prince Felipe.

The girls looked at each other.
They knew this was their moment.

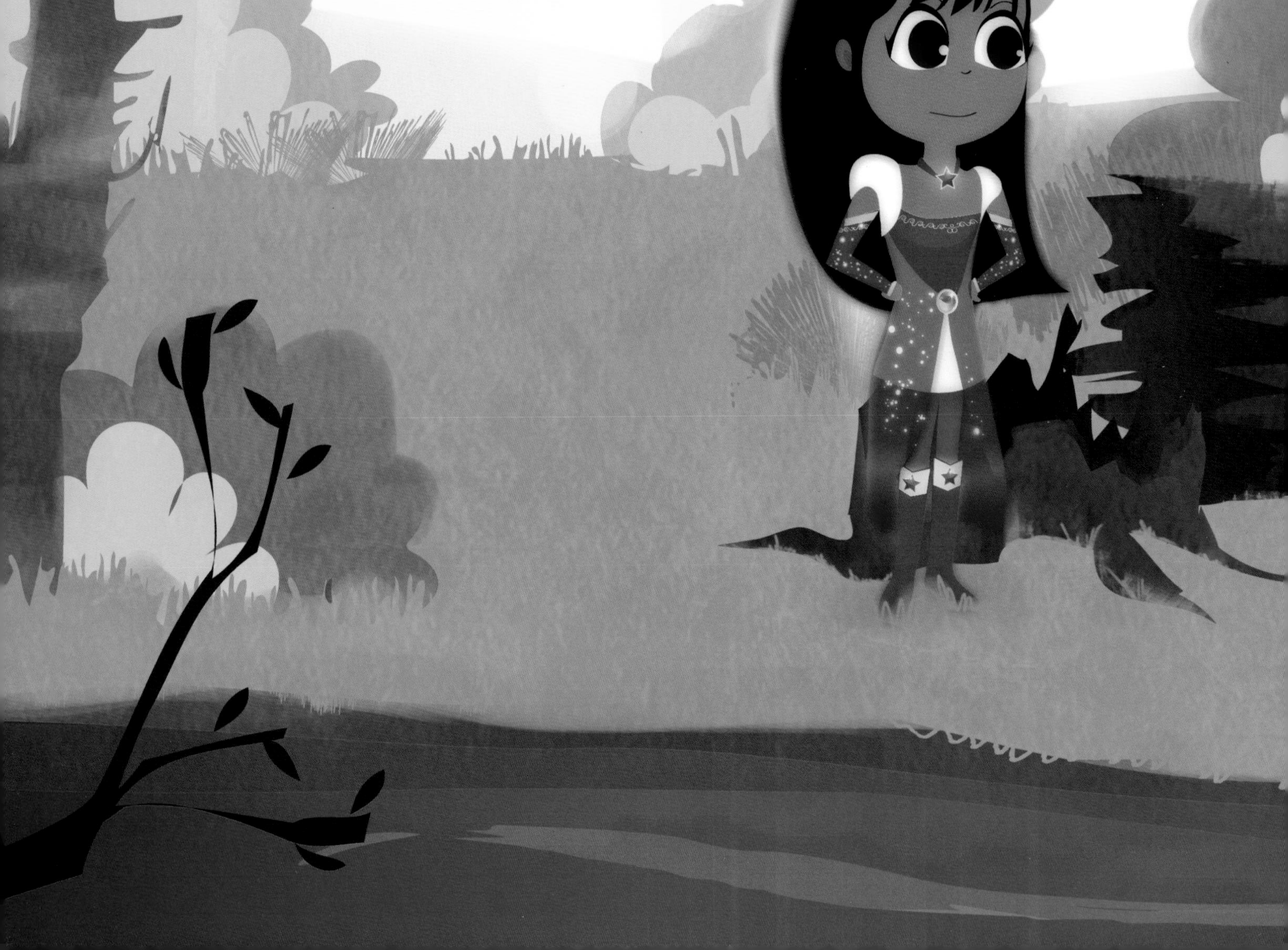

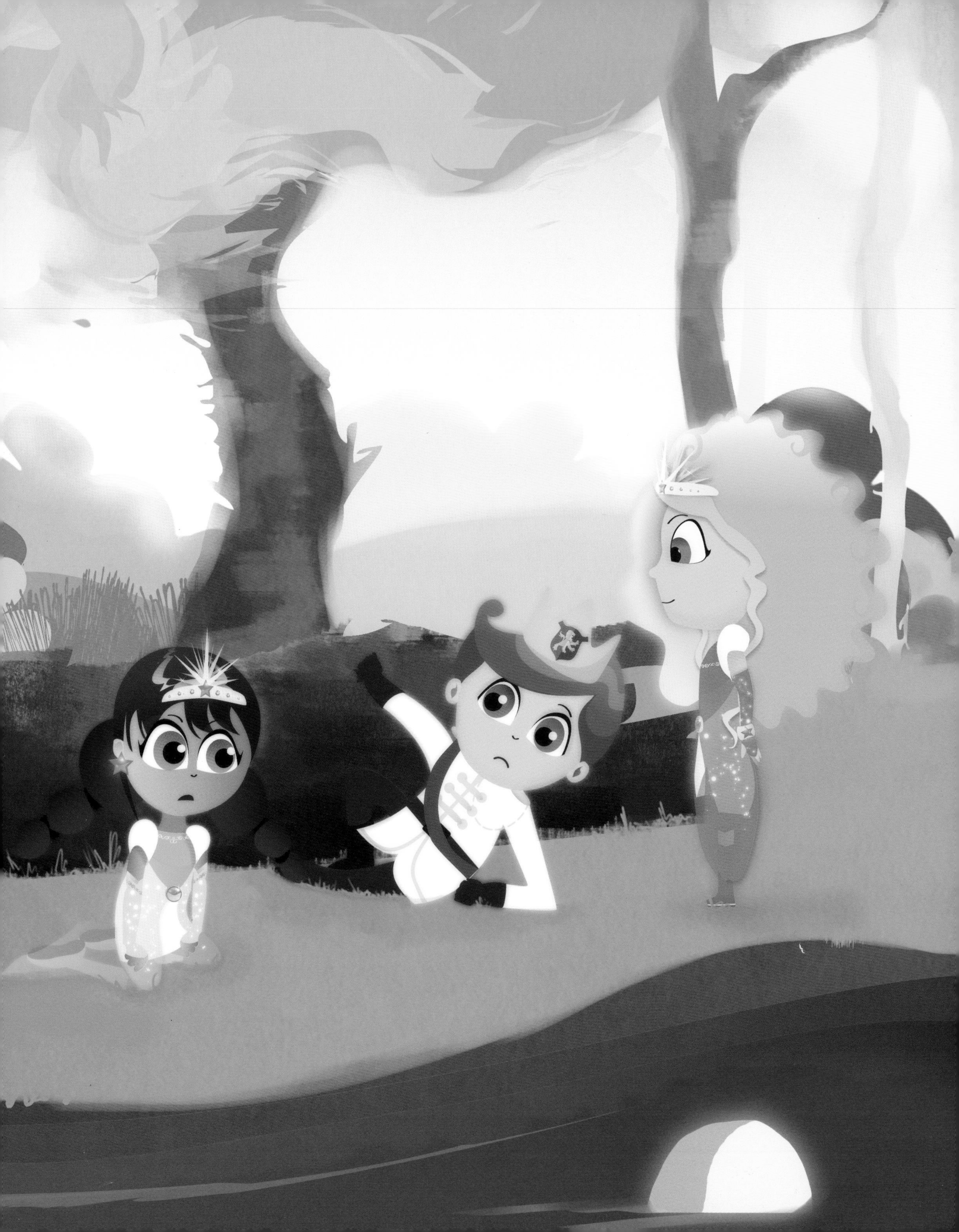

"I guess it's time to use our super powers," said Sammie. "I'm *strong*, so I'll move the tree!"

"I can *fly*. I'll take the Prince over the river," said Oceana.

"I'm *fast*, so I'll rush him home before it gets dark," chimed in Kinney.

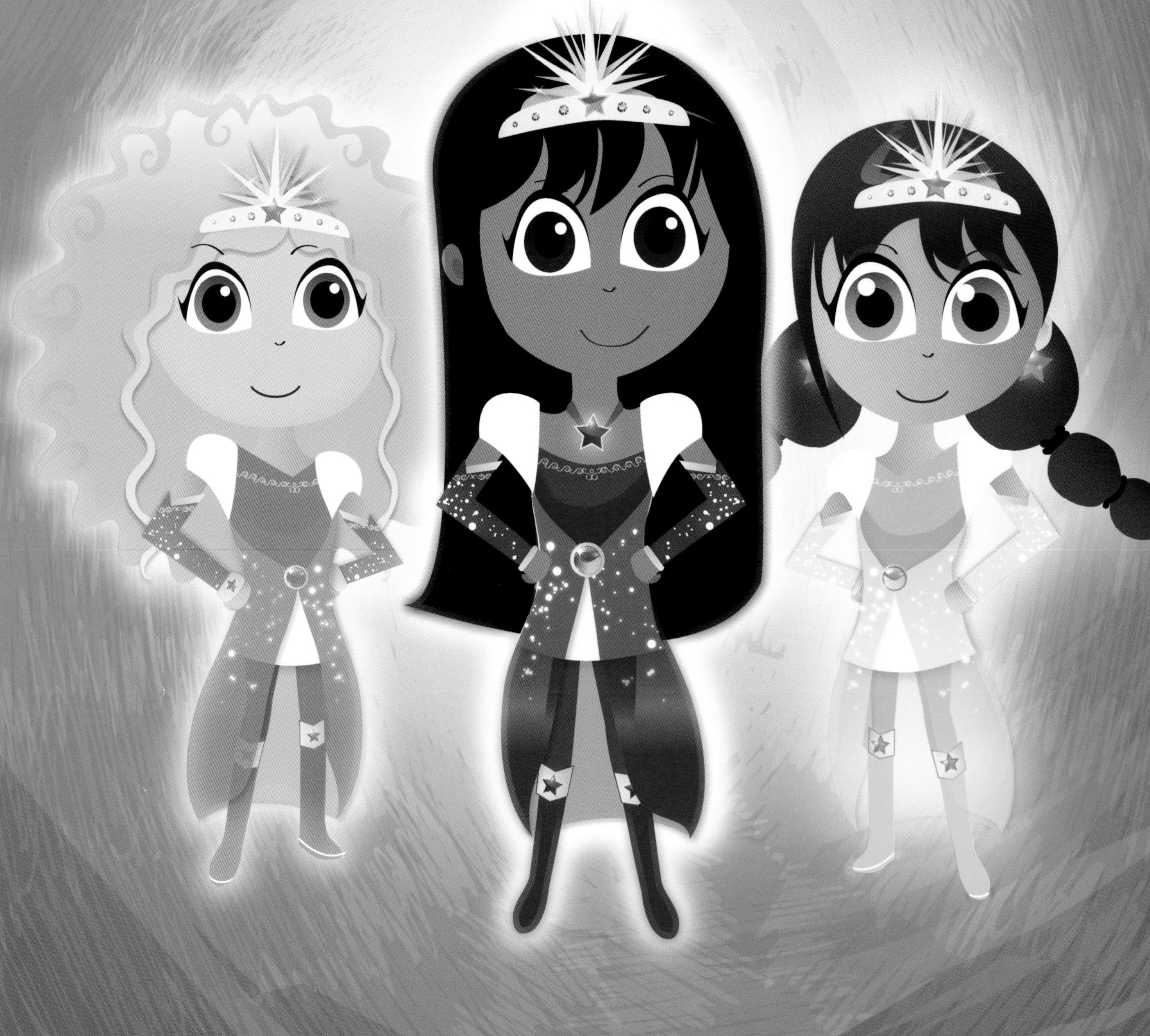

The girls sprang to action!

Sammie picked up the fallen tree like it was a tiny twig and moved it aside.

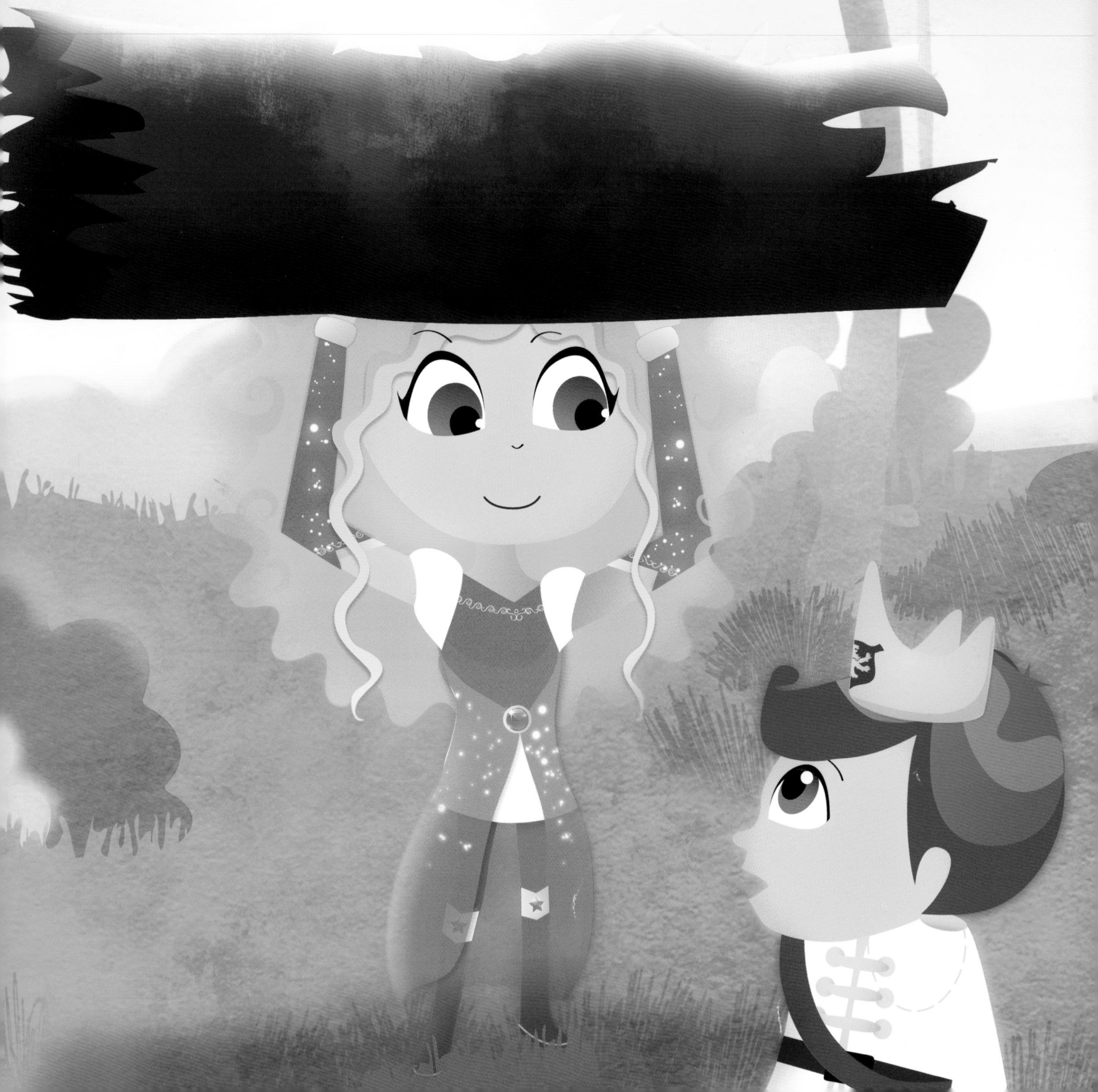

"Don't worry, Prince," said Oceana. "Hold my hand. I'll use my super flying powers to take you and Kinney to the other side!"

"Wait a second," said Prince Felipe, as he wiped tears from his eyes. "You're girls. Aren't I supposed to help you?"

"Excuse me?" said Kinney. "We're Super Duper Princess Heroes We're here to help everybody. Plus, who said girls weren't supposed to help boys?"

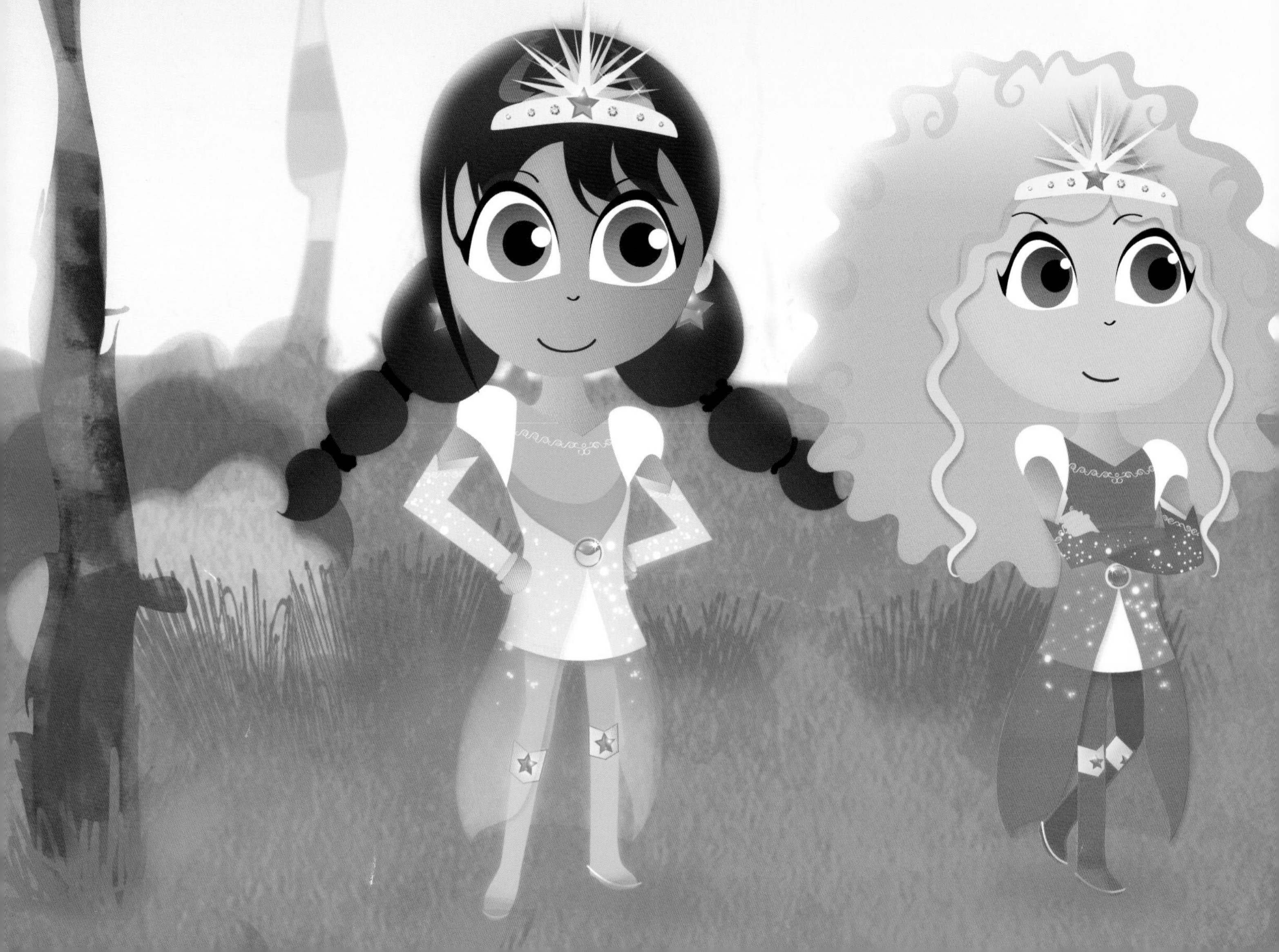

"But then will one of you want to marry me?" replied Prince Felipe. "Isn't that what princesses are supposed to do—marry princes?"

"You think that just because we're princesses all we want to do is marry you?" said Oceana. "No way! Listen, Prince, you might be royalty and everything, but we have way more important things to do than marrying you, like *saving the world*. Let's stop wasting time. Are you ready to go?"

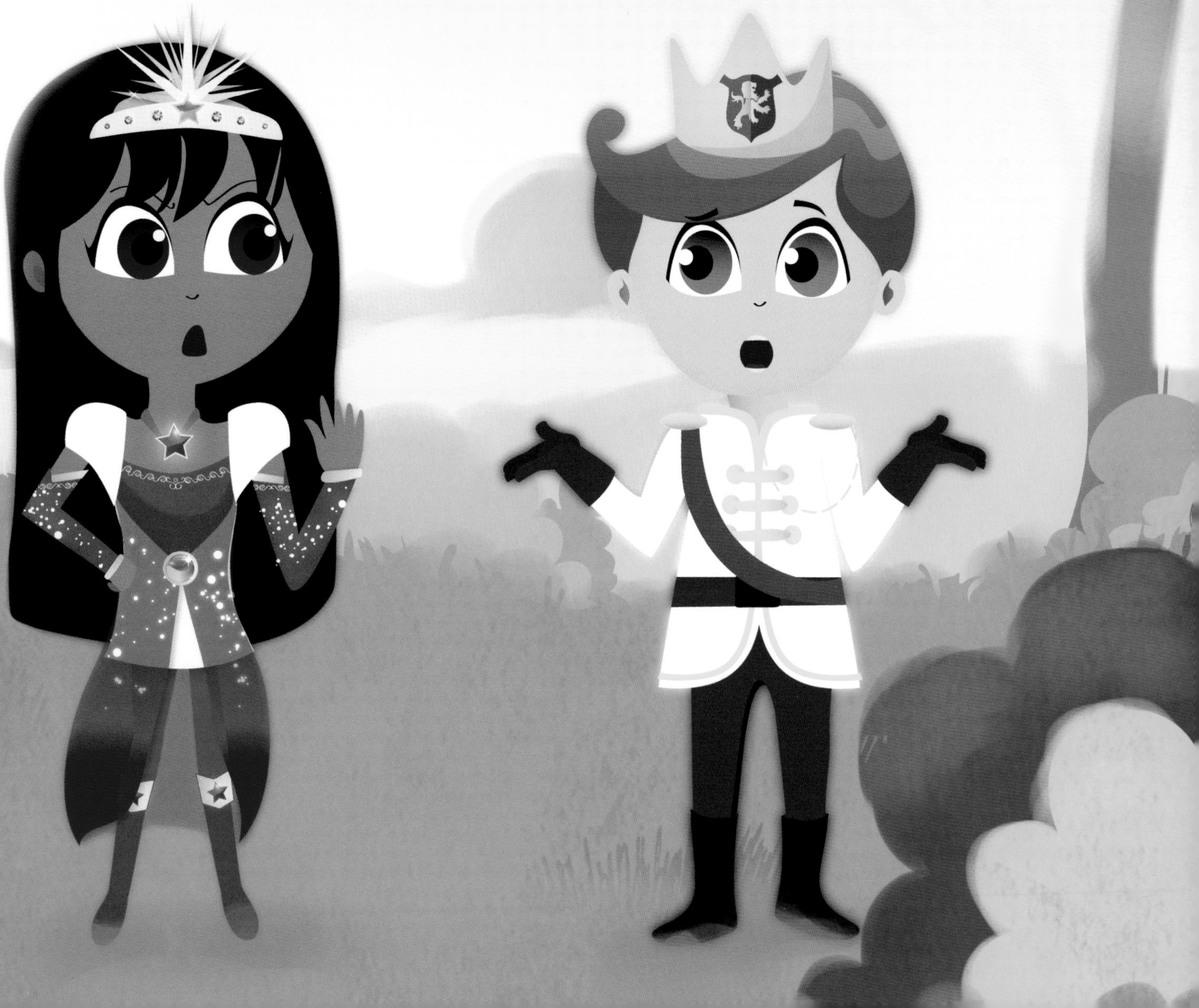

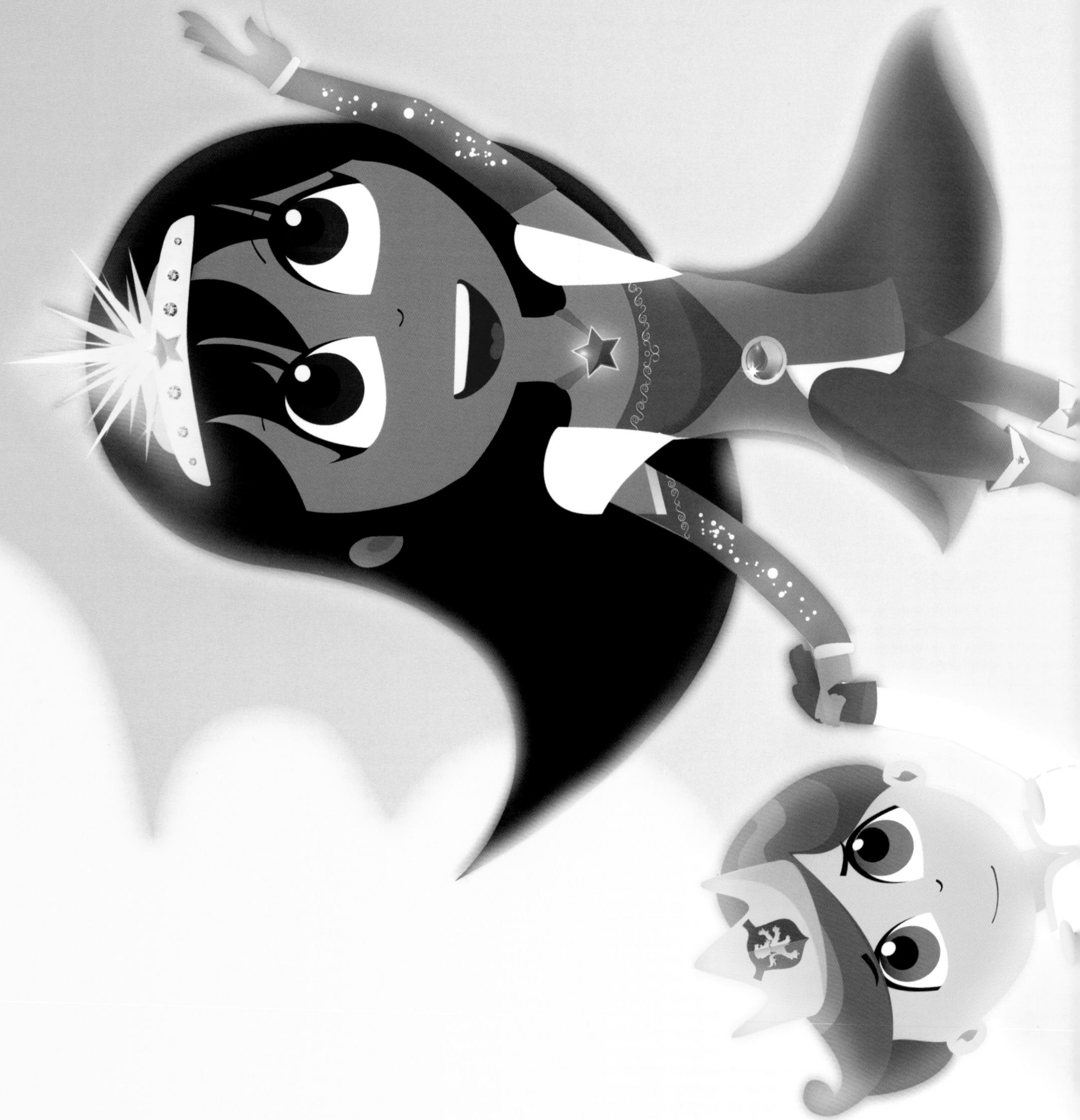

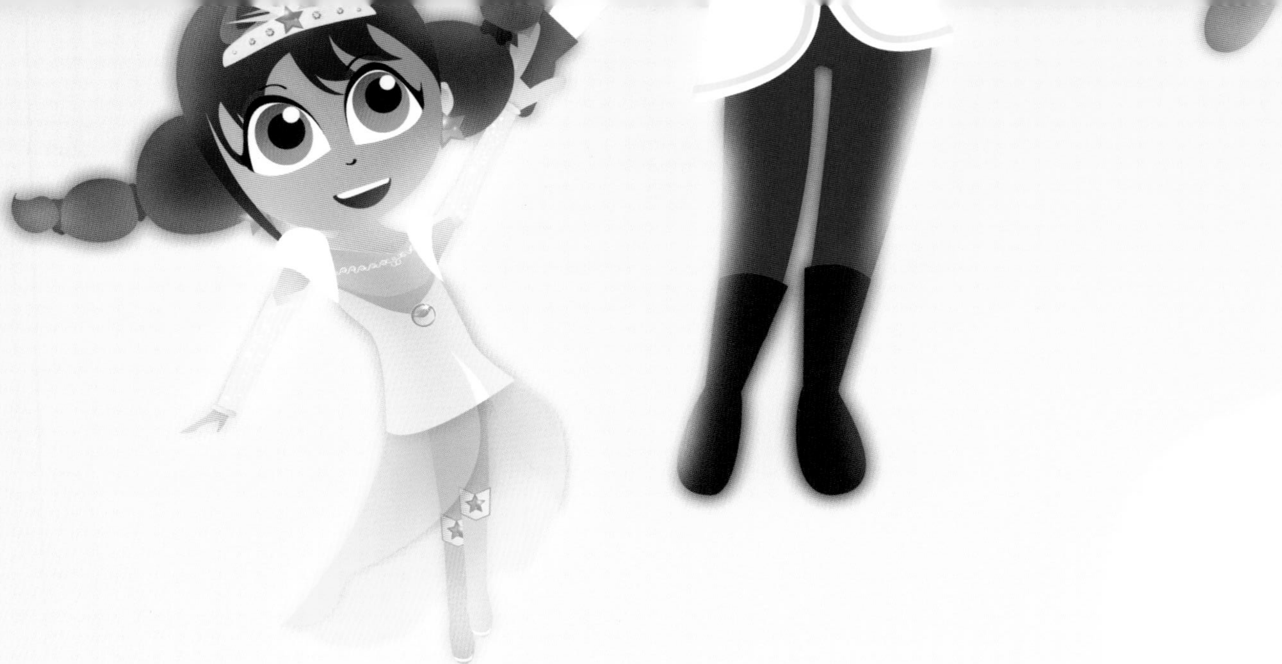

"Okay, let's go," said Prince Felipe. He was embarrassed, but he also was grateful for the girls' help.

Oceana flew the Prince and Kinney across the river.

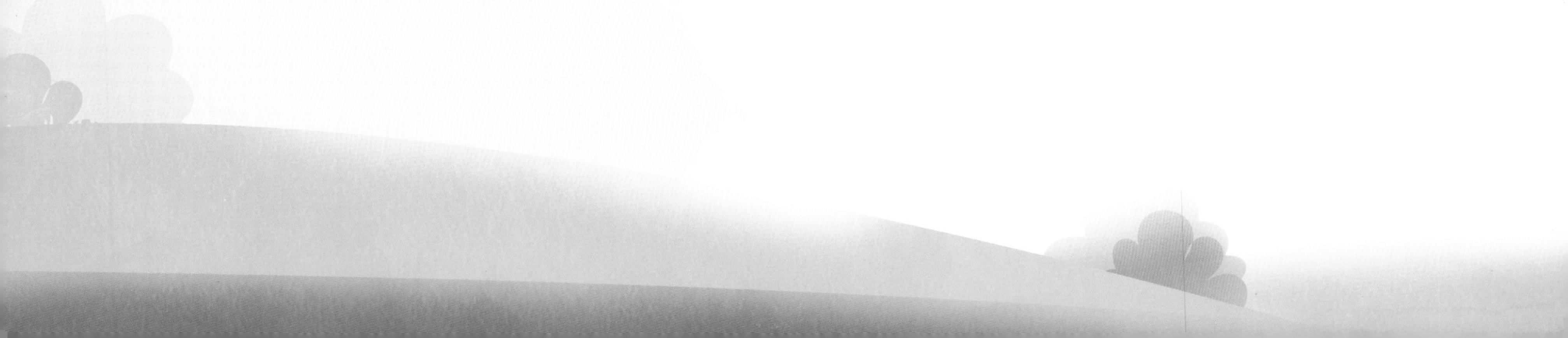

"Hold my hand and we'll run to your castle," said Kinney.

Prince Felipe pointed toward his home and held Kinney's hand. She ran so fast his legs barely touched the ground.

She dropped him off, returned to the river, and flew back with Oceana.

Prince Felipe, meanwhile, was safe. As his mommy tended to his injuries, he told her about the extraordinary girls he just met. Soon, the entire kingdom would hear about the story.

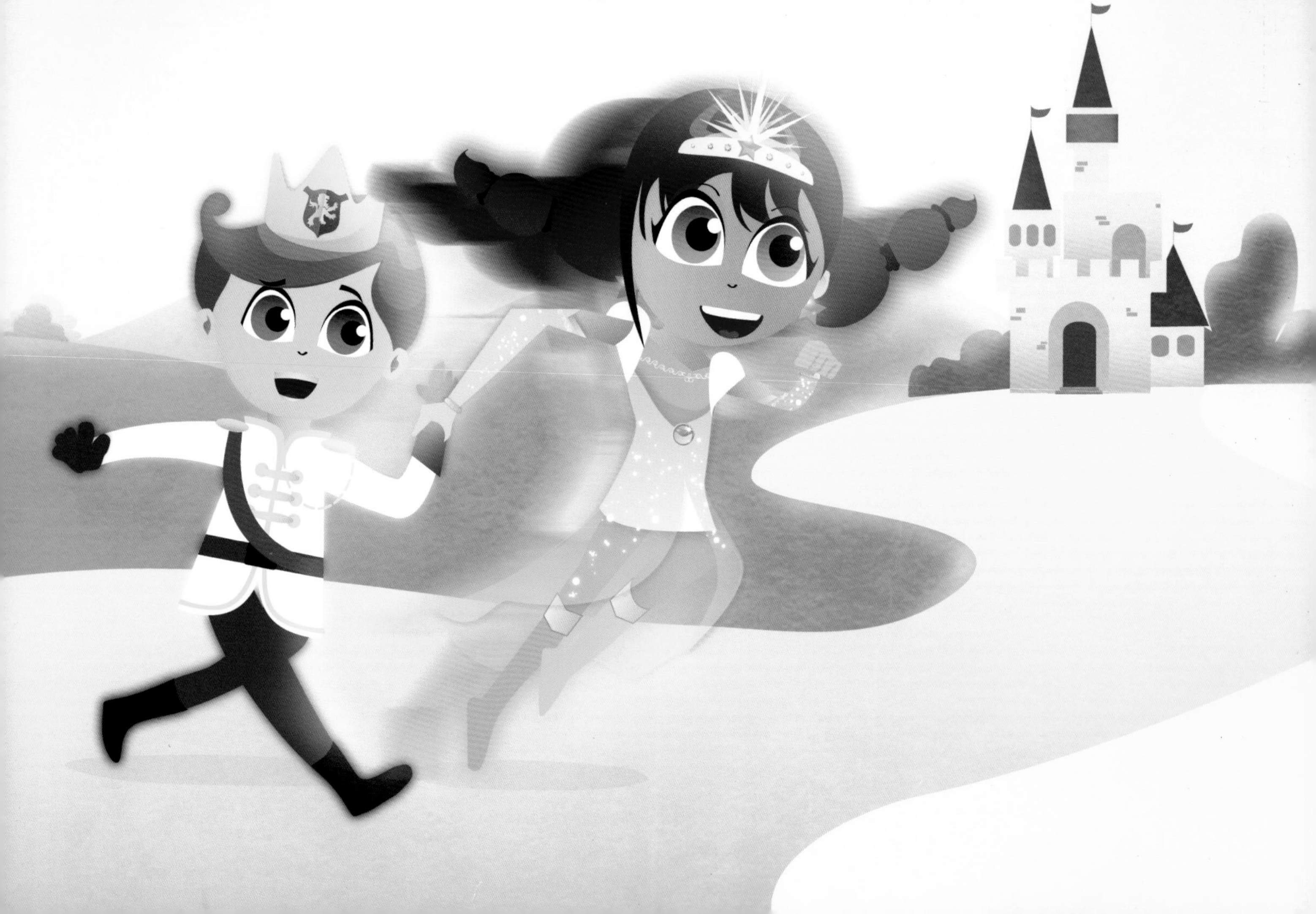

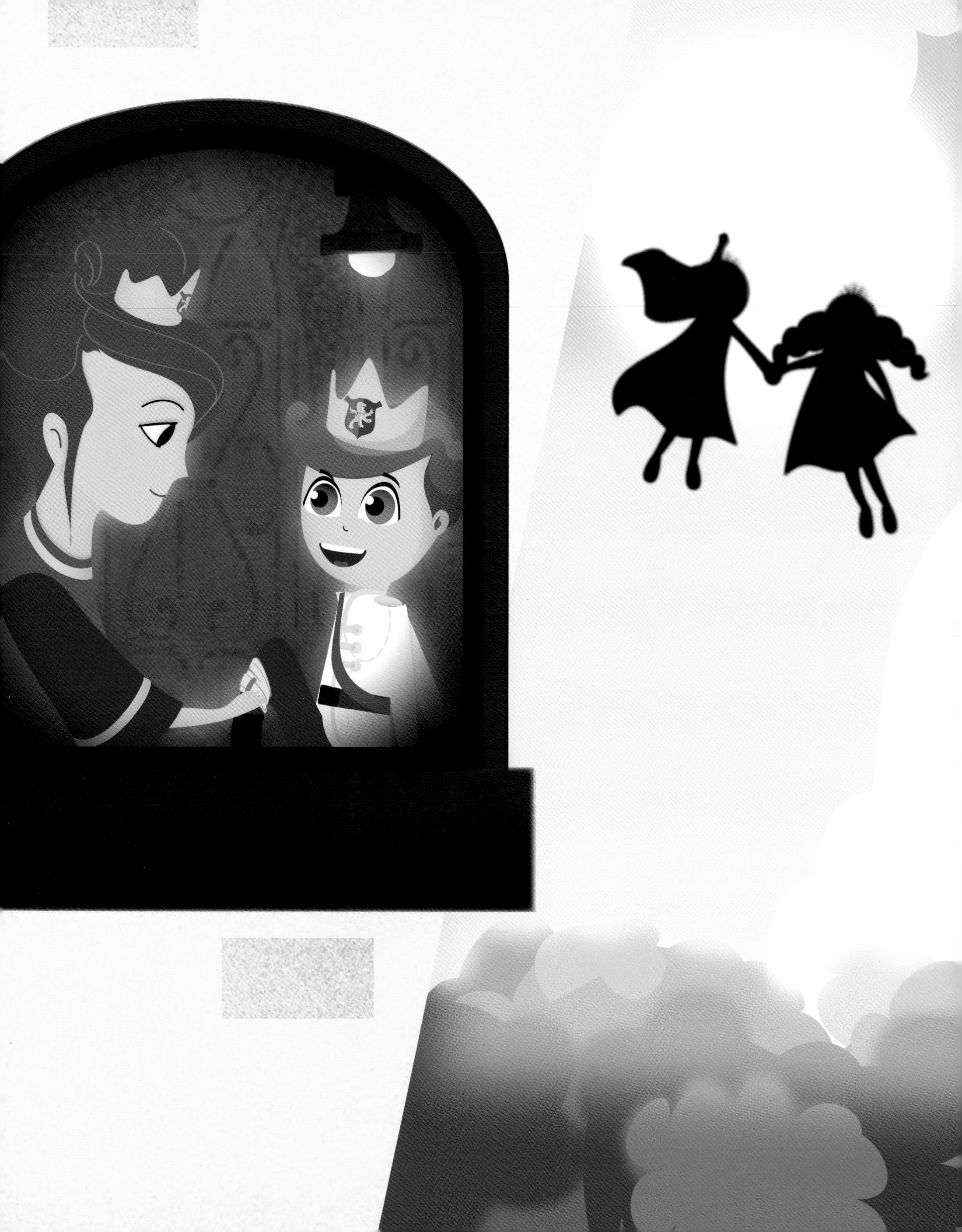

Kinney, Oceana, and Sammie walked home together under the enchanting dusk sky. They removed their tiaras and transformed back into regular girls.

They talked about their new amazing abilities. Although having super powers was a lot of fun, it also came with a lot of responsibility. But the girls realized that this was their chance to make a difference in their world.

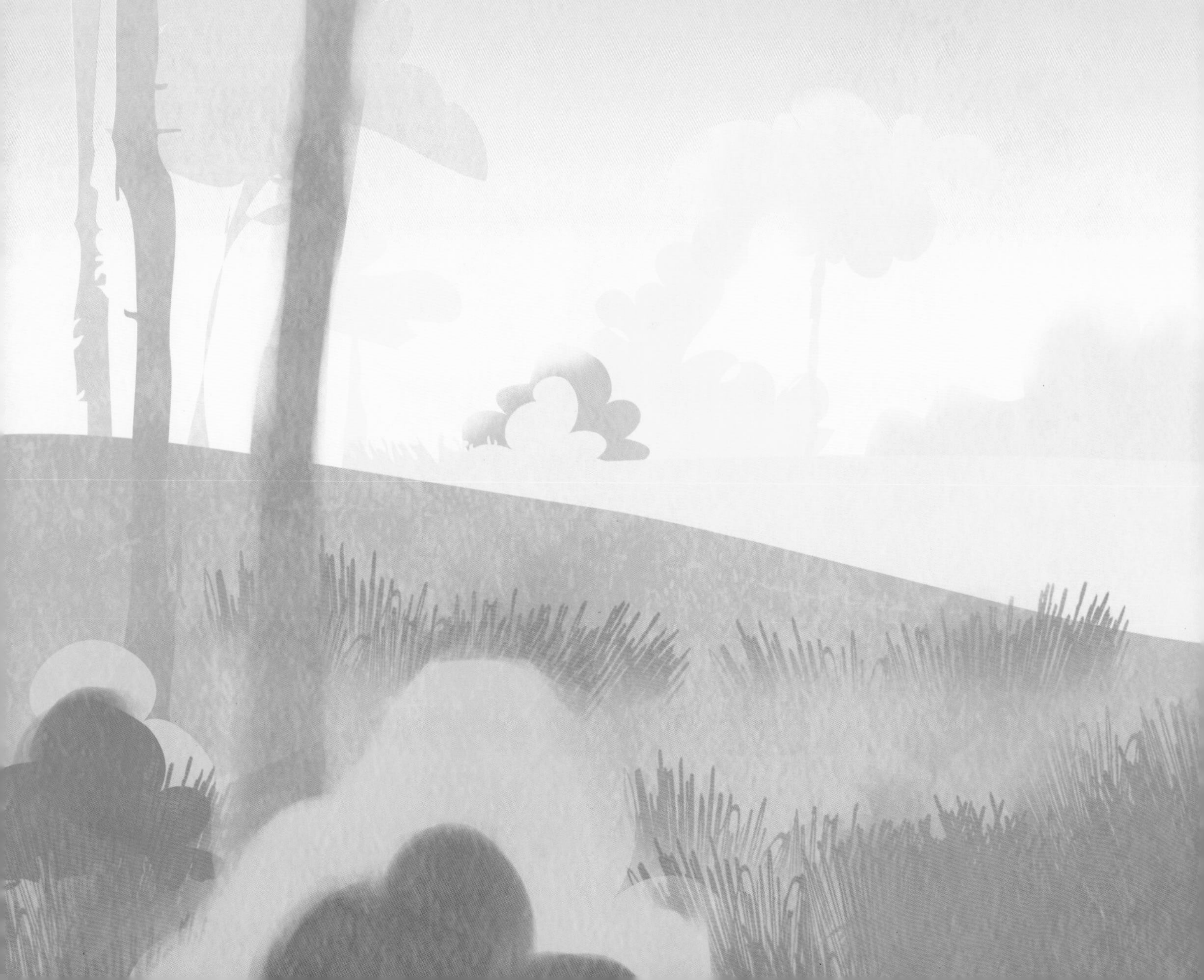

Just then, they heard another *scream!* Someone needed help. It was time for . . .

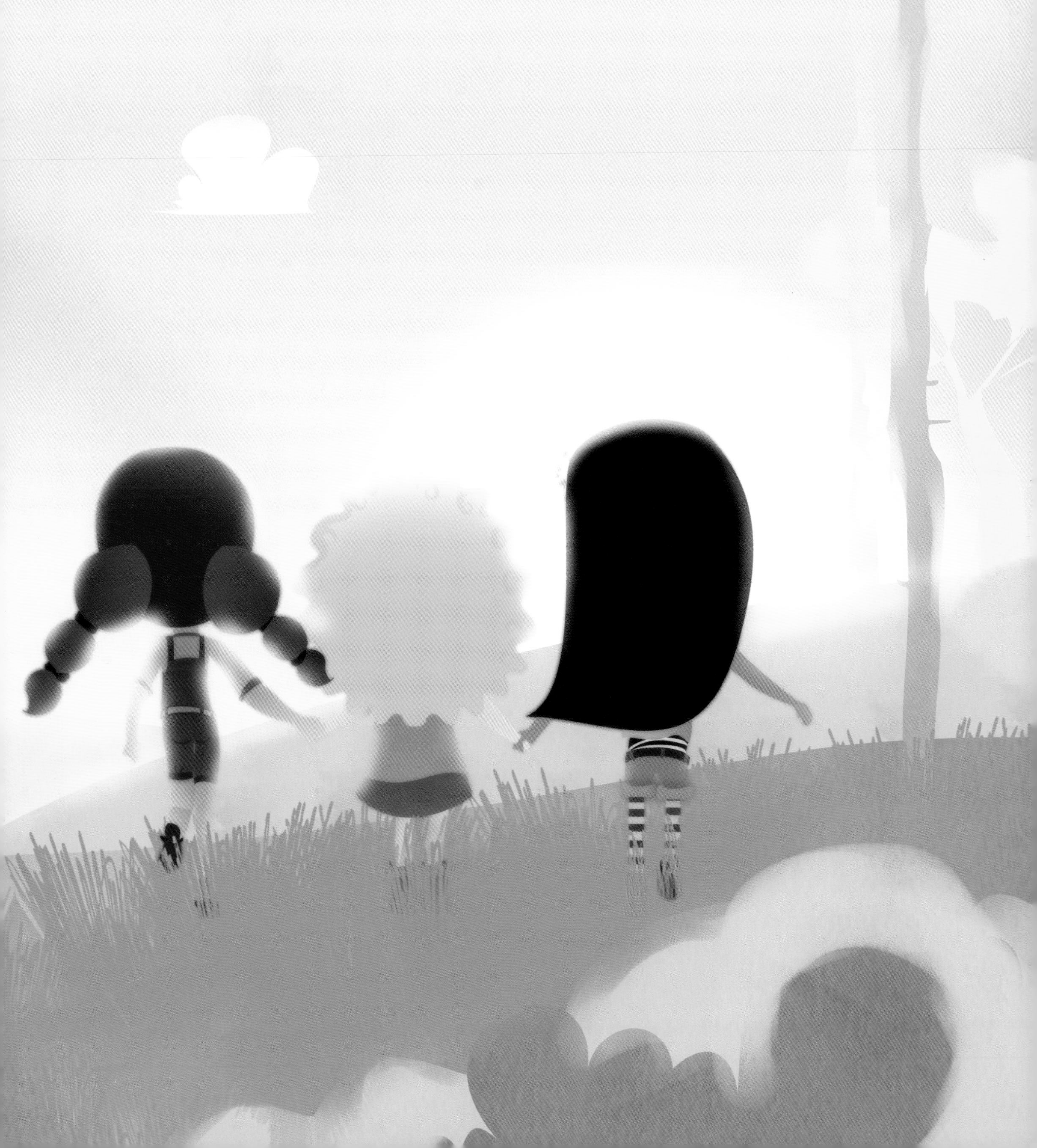

...The SUPER DUPER PRINCESS Heroes

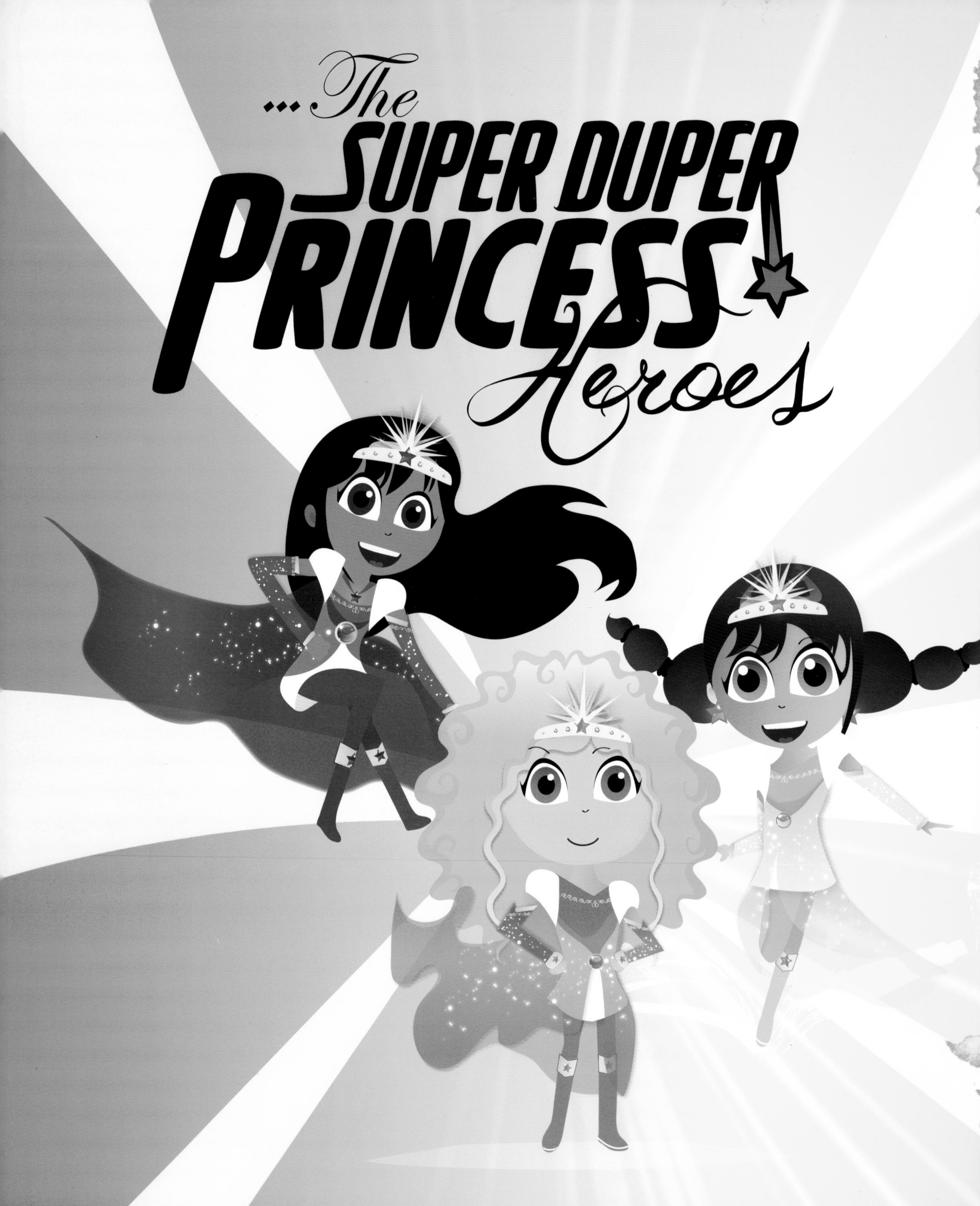